Strange Things

Also By Dustin Warburton

"Reading Dustin Warburton's "Taste" is a bit like having your mind run through a wood chipper praying you'll be able to put all the pieces back together in the end....smart, scary stuff."

- Reggie Bannister

Available at www.tastethebook.com and select retailers.

STRANGE THINGS

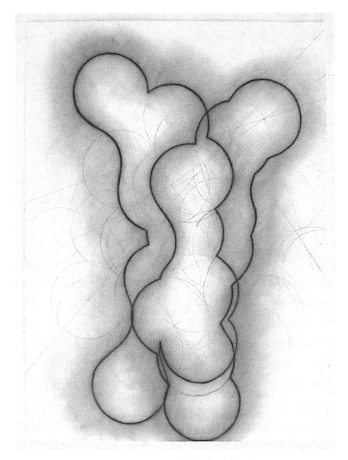

NEIGHBORHOOD PUBLISHERS

VERNONT

2021

WRITEN BY DUSTIN WARBURTON

NEIGHBORHOOD
PUBLISHERS

Printed in The United States of America

This book is dedicated to the memory of Claude Moore
July 20th, 1922 – August 20th, 2007

About the Author

Dustin Warburton grew up in a small rural community in upstate N.Y. At an early age he was interested in writing fiction and tried to publish his first book at the age of 12. In 1999 he was published for the first time and accepted into the New England Young Writers Conference in Middlebury, Vermont. Dustin moved to Vermont in 2002 with his wife and child and currently works as an English Teacher in a private school. He graduated from Union Institute and University with his B.A. in Writing and Literature and published his first horror novel in 2005 with his longtime friend, Nathan Gorman. This is his second book.

www.dustinwarburton.com

About the Artist:
Craig Stockwell

Craig Stockwell has been an artist since finishing his studies at Dartmouth College and Rhode Island School of Design in 1975. At RISD he studied with Glass artist Dale Chihuly and went on to do work in glass in Minneapolis, Boulder and Boston. His work moved on to conceptually based sculptural installations and was shown in New York, notably at PS. That particular installation was chosen from PS1 and included in a show of eight sculptures (including Louise Bourgeois, Mark Di Suvero, Jack Ferrara, Alan Saret, and et.al.) The New York was widely reviewed including the New York Times, The Village Voice, Newsday, and the Soho News. After many years in New York, Stockwell moved to Spain with his young family in 1986. In 1988 they settled in New Hampshire where Stockwell made in intentional decision to confine his work to the restrictions of painting as a method of creating a sustainable daily practice. He received an MFA Degree from Vermont College in 2000. Stockwell lives in Keene, N.H. with his wife and three daughters. He teaches at Keene State College and Vermont College.

www.craigstockwell.com

About the Artist:
Stephen Blickenstaff

Stephen Blickenstaff is an incredible artist with an unusual style. He is most known for drawing the cover for the Cramps album, "Bad Music for Bad People," which was drawn on Halloween day, 1983. Stephen's artwork has graced the pages of Guitar World Magazine, and has been exhibited across the country in numerous Art Galleries. Stephen attends conventions throughout the Northeast while exhibiting his work to tens of thousands. His work can be seen at www.Stephenblickenstaff.com

www.stephenblickenstaff.com

About the Artist:
John Edward Bonaventure Federowicz

John Edward Bonaventure Federowicz, better known as Jon Ed Bon Fed, always the freelance illustrator has journeyed (and journaled) from the nail-biting world of advertising to the hair-pulling world of educating. BonFed's art is rooted in the desire to communicate and share. From caricaturing to capturing lifetimes, to watercolors capturing the American spirit, to whimsical art where tears capture paint, he now invites you into his proverbial sketchbook, "Where the World is Drawn Together."

www.bonfed.com

About the Artist:
Frank Russo

Frank Russo has been an artist for many years. His work can be seen in numerous Art Galleries across the country. He currently runs and owns MF Gallery on 157 Rivington Street, NYC. His gallery features hundreds of artists interested in the horror genre. For information about this artist and his Gallery, visit www.mfgallery.net

www.mfgallery.net

About the Artist:
Jay Trefethen

Jay Trefethen is a self-taught artist currently living in Vermont. He was inspired to pursue an art career by his late uncle, Clint Trefethen who was an accomplished graphic designer, illustrator and oil painter. Jay is following in his footsteps with his own pen and ink illustrations and oil paintings.

www.nightairstudios.com

About the Artist:
Nathan Gorman

Nathan Gorman grew up in a rural community in upstate N.Y. His family currently owns the General Store in town. Nathan's artistic ability was evident at an early age, as he often cut up newspapers and magazines to create portraits. Or he would make stone chairs out of the crumbling rock walls behind his parent's farmhouse. After attending Art School in Pittsburgh, Nathan moved back to N.Y. and has worked as a chef in Ithaca and Binghamton N.Y. for many years. His work has been exhibited in Art Galleries in New York City and London. Nathan illustrated the horror novel, "Taste," in 2005. For more information about this artist contact BareBones Publishing.

www.tastethebook.com

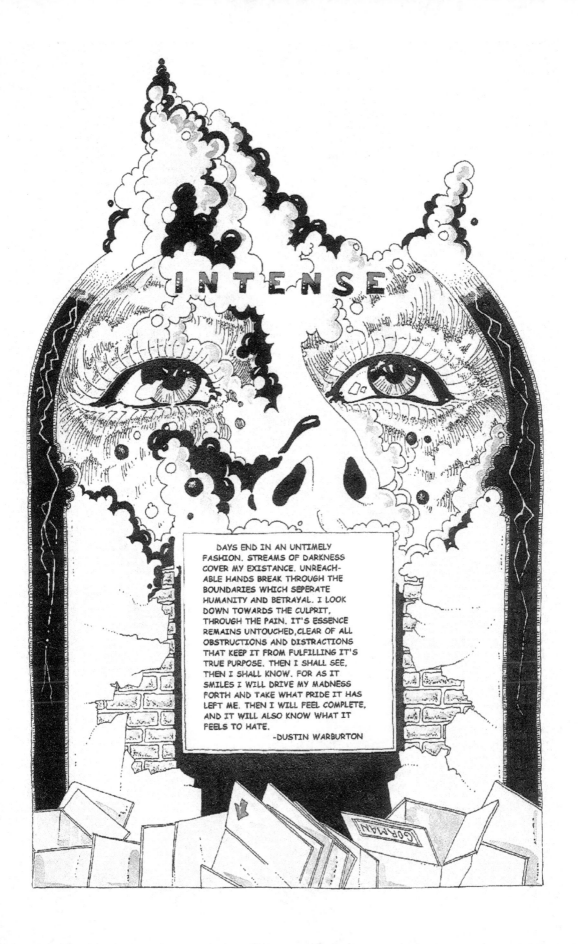

CHAPTER 1

PALE BLUE SUIT

Pale Blue Suit

Written by Dustin Warburton

Illustrated by Jay Trefethen

"I feel the wickedness upon me," the shadowy figure whispered as it prowled among the bushes and trees of

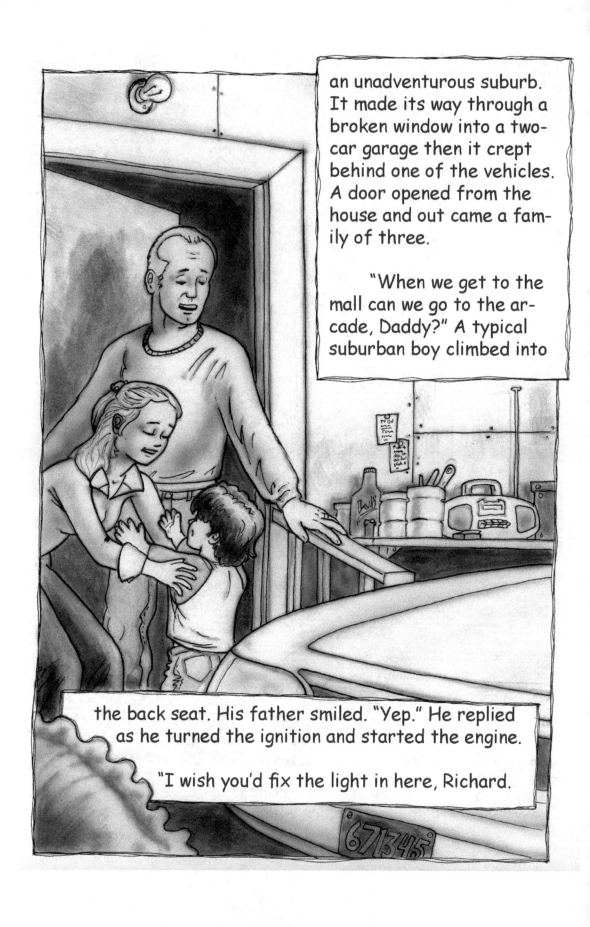

an unadventurous suburb. It made its way through a broken window into a two-car garage then it crept behind one of the vehicles. A door opened from the house and out came a family of three.

"When we get to the mall can we go to the arcade, Daddy?" A typical suburban boy climbed into

the back seat. His father smiled. "Yep." He replied as he turned the ignition and started the engine.

"I wish you'd fix the light in here, Richard.

A typical suburban housewife buckled her seat belt.
"I practically sprained my ankle on a skateboard just
walking to the car."

   "Yeah, you're right. I'll have to get down to the
hardware store one of these days." Richard picked up
the remote to the garage door and pushed one of the

triangular buttons. The door opened, tilting shadows
across the walls on either side of the car. The moon
lit the inside of the garage as the door rose higher.

   "You've been saying that for weeks," his wife
said. Richard turned his head, smiled, and leaned in to
give her a kiss.

"Dad, let's go to the arcade." Both husband and wife looked toward their child and embraced his innocence. Richard shifted into reverse and backed the car out of the garage. He let the car roll into the street, into drive, and clicked the remote control again. The garage door was half shut when something triggered his attention. A shadowy white figure stood inside

the garage. "What the hell?" Richard's foot stomped on the brake pedal, jolting the car to a stop. The boy laughed as Richard unbuckled his seatbelt, his hand on the door.

"Richard, what on earth are you doing?" his wife cried out. Richard opened the door. "You stay here, Irene. Lock the doors and get into the driver's seat.

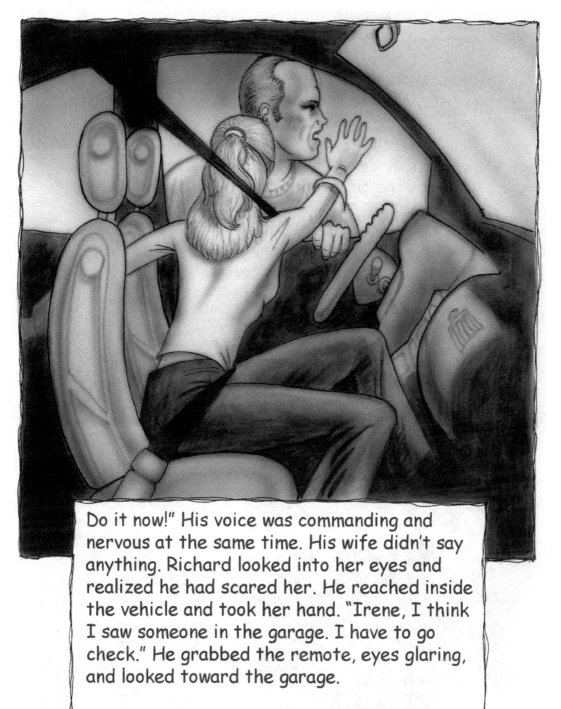

Do it now!" His voice was commanding and nervous at the same time. His wife didn't say anything. Richard looked into her eyes and realized he had scared her. He reached inside the vehicle and took her hand. "Irene, I think I saw someone in the garage. I have to go check." He grabbed the remote, eyes glaring, and looked toward the garage.

"Richard, let's go get the police. Richard, please." She pleaded in fear.

"I've got to check," Richard said.

Irene reached out to Richard, grabbing his hand. The boy remained silent in the back seat, wide eyed and taking it all in.

"It isn't worth it. There's nothing in there that we can't replace. Please, Richard, let's just go get the police." Her voice cracked. She gripped his hand even tighter.

"Lock the door. I'll be right back." Richard pulled his hand out of his wife's grip and started walking toward his home. Irene tried to keep a calm face so their son wouldn't be

frightened.

"Where's Daddy going, Mom?" The little boy rummaged through the toys in the backseat, acting as if he knew nothing about what was going on.

"Daddy forgot something, sweetheart. He'll be right back." A teardrop ran down her cheek as she looked out the window, watching Richard fade from view in the night air.

As Richard approached the foot of his driveway, he stopped and looked back toward the car, then proceeded up the gravel way with caution. Television shows such as Cops and America's Most Wanted

flooded his thoughts. He wondered if there was a thief hiding in the garage, waiting to loot and pillage his home? Or was there a psycho-driven maniac with a switchblade, ready to carve some new flesh, waiting for him to open the garage door? Or maybe his eyes had deceived him and there was nothing more than a hungry cat scurrying among the trash bags. Richard wasn't taking any chances. He stooped down and picked up an aluminum baseball bat that was lying in the grass. His son must have left it there. Normally Richard would have scolded his son about leaving things outside, but not this time.

"Thank God he doesn't listen to me." Richard rose with the shiny bat in his hand. Now that he had a weapon that could bring down any man, he triggered the remote control and said, "Here goes nothing." He dropped the remote and gripped the bat with both hands.

The garage door opened and Richard felt the sweat dripping from his forehead. He was prepared to swing for a homerun. Nothing was going to escape the wrath of that baseball bat, especially when fear motivated the batter. As soon as the door opened all the way, Richard ran into the garage. He walked around the other car, examining the inside and underneath as well, then approached the door

to his house. He tried the doorknob, but it was still locked. Then reality hit him. "What am I doing?" He tossed the bat into a pile of junk and walked out of the garage. He picked up the remote control and pressed the button as he continued walking down the driveway toward the road.

He turned to look at the garage door one last time. He could see nothing but darkness inside the garage this time. He shook his head in disgust. "Too much coffee." He stepped into the paved street and kept walking.

As Richard approached the rear of the car, he stopped dead in his tracks. There was something in the back window. Its face pressed against the rear window. White. Sickly. A ghoul of a face. Its lips smeared yellowish-red saliva over the glass. Its skin looked thin and tightly wrapped over a sharp bony skull. The eyes were pure black. Doomed.

Richard was locked in place. Then he started trembling. The car started to move down the street, away from Richard. He shook himself out of his nightmarish coma and suddenly realized what he was witnessing.

"No!" he screamed. He ran after the car, his

family still inside. The car accelerated, driving farther and farther out of reach. "No!" Richard cried. He continued as fast as his body would carry him. As the car drove away, the ghoulish face was still visible. Its ghastly image locked in Richard's brain. Within moments, his wife and son were gone.

Richard kept running. He was found the next morning nearly ten miles away. Police responded to a call from a concerned family who found a stranger sleeping in their yard. Richard was taken into custody and placed inside an interrogation room. He told the police the bizarre events of the night before. He didn't understand why the police weren't being more cooperative. He began to get angry.

A tall, slender man wearing a pale blue suit entered the room. He held a folder in his left hand. Richard bit his lip. "We have to find them now!" he screamed. The man in the pale blue suit slammed his left hand on the table in front of Richard, spilling the contents of the folder. Richard's eyes took in the photographs that covered the table. Picture after picture of his bloody car. Richard's

mouth hung open. His face turned white. The man in the pale blue suit slammed his other hand on the table.

"You're God-damn right. We do have to find your wife and son don't we?" The detective's eyes were raging.

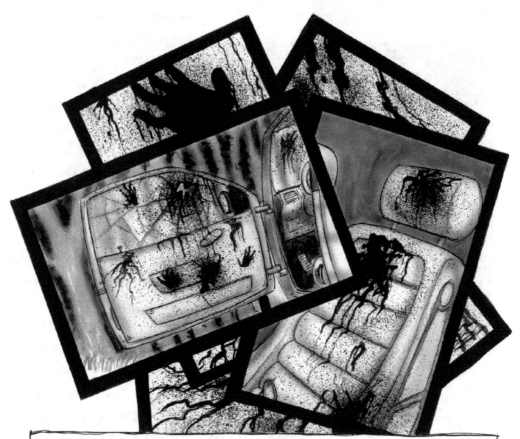

"Oh my God," Richard breathed as he looked at photo after photo and slipped from his chair to the floor. He began to vomit.

"Oh, Christ. Somebody get a bucket," the detective called out. Richard started hyperventilating. He crawled to the corner of the room, taking refuge there with his back against the wall. Two more police officers came into the room, one of them carrying a bucket.

The detective closed in Richard. "Where are they, Richard? Why did you do it, Richard? You're a sick fuck and you're going to burn for this, Richard!" The detective stared at him. Richard blinked and tried to say something.

"Hey, wait a minute. I think he's got something to say." The detective knelt down on the vomit-slick floor and tried to make eye contact. "What's that, Richard?"

"She was wrong," Richard said. His body shivered and twitched like a mechanical toy gone haywire.

The detective looked toward the other police officers. "Who was wrong, your wife?" The three men, eager to break the case in the early hours of investigation, were anticipating a confession. Richard wiped his eyes and folded his arms, resting them on his knees.

"Come on now, Richard, tell us what your wife did wrong. Its OK, everything is going to be all right." The detective used a soothing voice, easing the impending confession. Richard lifted his head and took a deep breath. He turned and faced the detective.

"She said it wasn't worth it. That there was nothing we had that we couldn't replace. She was wrong."

CHAPTER 2

KILLA DWARF

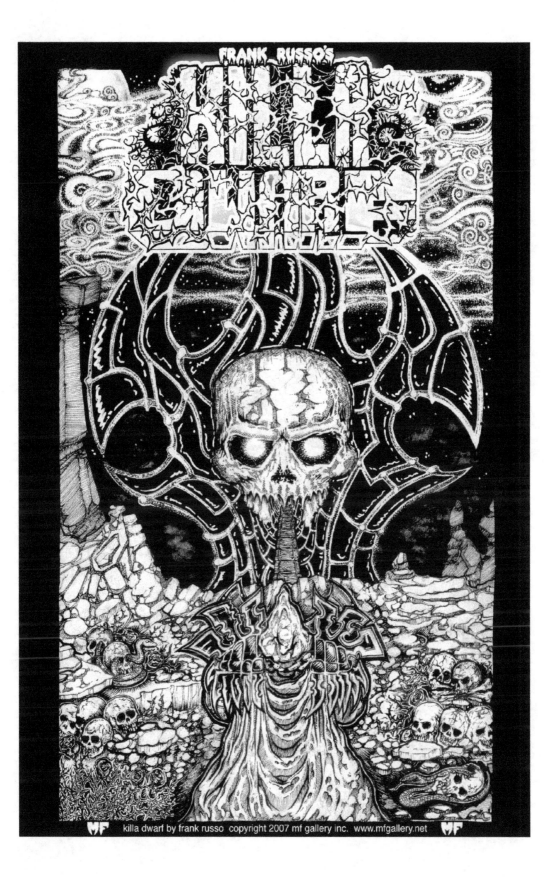

killa dwarf by frank russo copyright 2007 mf gallery inc. www.mfgallery.net

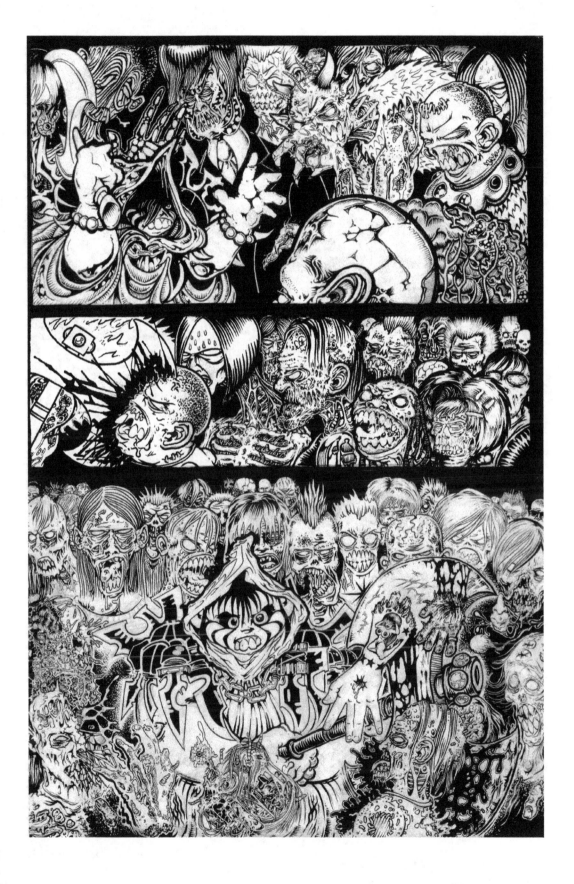

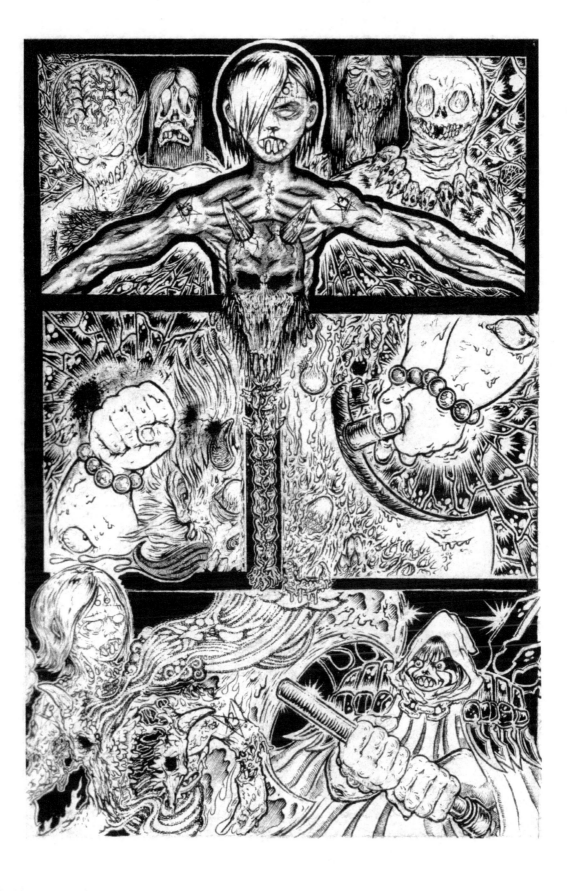

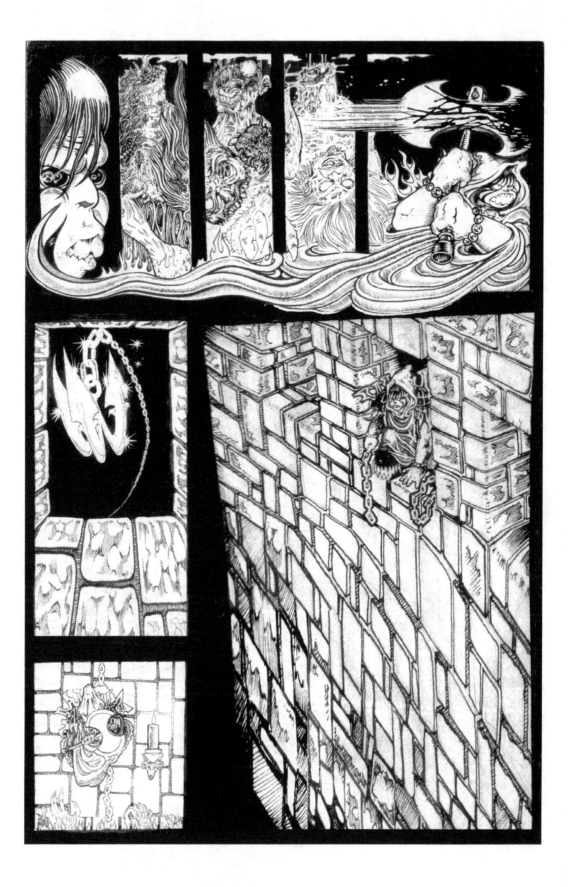

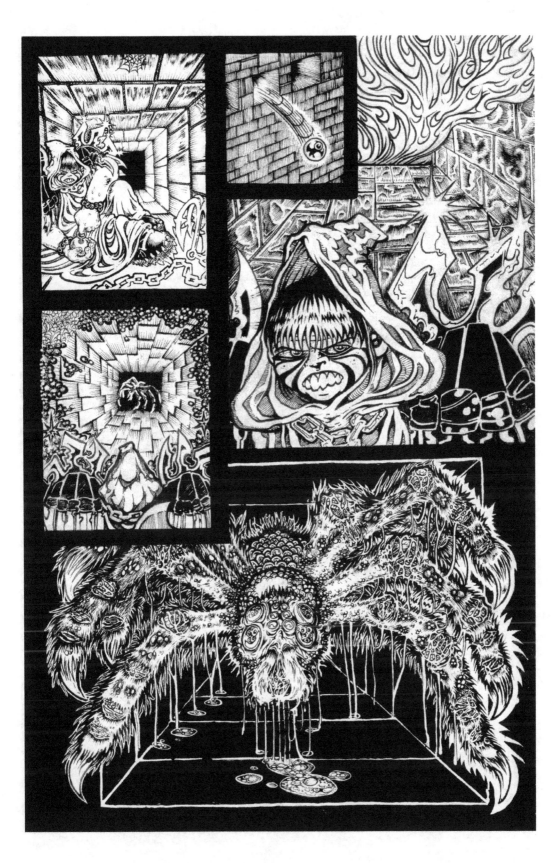

CHAPTER 3

316

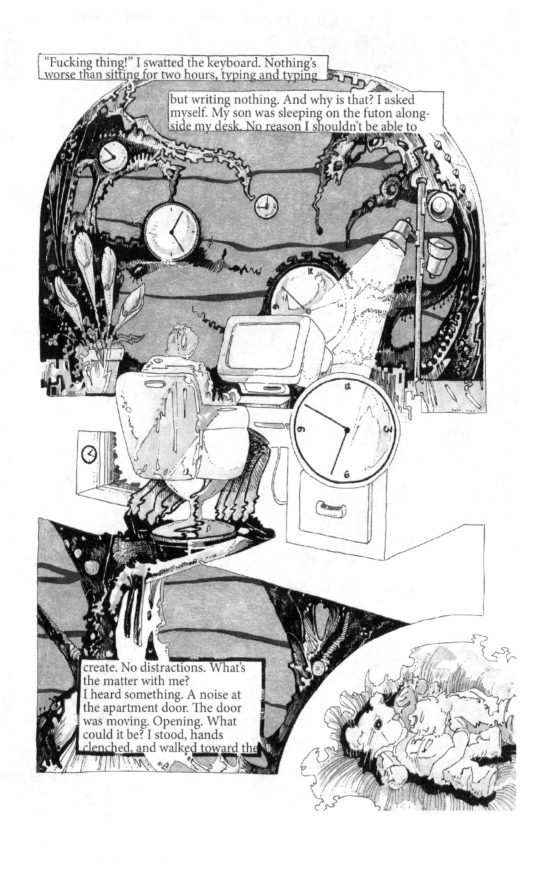

"Fucking thing!" I swatted the keyboard. Nothing's worse than sitting for two hours, typing and typing

but writing nothing. And why is that? I asked myself. My son was sleeping on the futon alongside my desk. No reason I shouldn't be able to

create. No distractions. What's the matter with me?
I heard something. A noise at the apartment door. The door was moving. Opening. What could it be? I stood, hands clenched, and walked toward the

intruder. Someone was on the other side, pushing the door open.

I slammed the door and looked out the peephole. No one.

"I want my mommy," a little voice cried from outside.

I knew that voice. It was the neighbor's kid. His apartment was down the stairs and to the left. Kid must have wandered up without his mother seeing him. I re-

turned to the computer as the three-year-old continued to pout. "Kid's mother should know where he is. I'm not bringing him

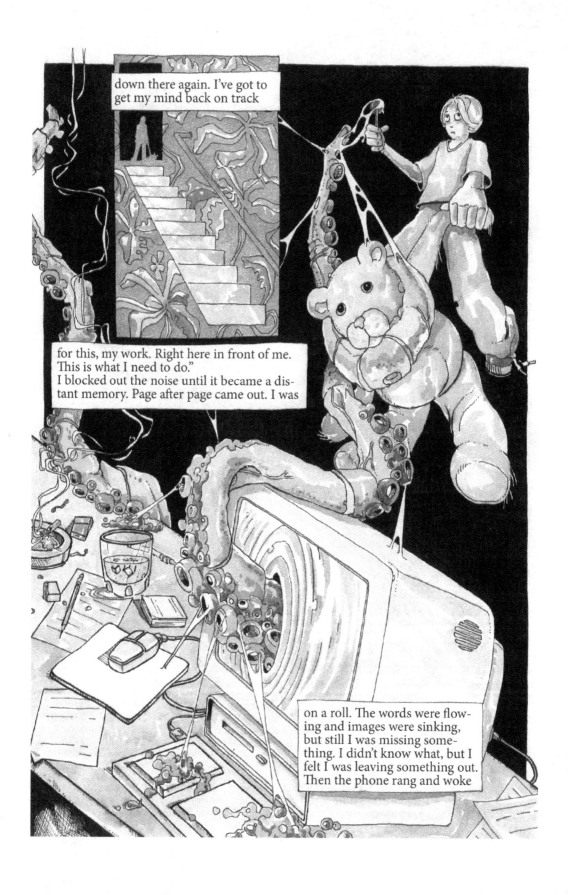

down there again. I've got to get my mind back on track

for this, my work. Right here in front of me. This is what I need to do."
I blocked out the noise until it became a distant memory. Page after page came out. I was

on a roll. The words were flowing and images were sinking, but still I was missing something. I didn't know what, but I felt I was leaving something out. Then the phone rang and woke

me from my daze.
"Hello?" No answer. I hung it up. Then screams from outside filled the air. I hurried to the window and looked out. There she was. The kid's mother. Ranting and raving about something in the parking lot. I stepped back and went out into the hallway. At the stairwell

I looked down and knew what had happened. I knew what I had done. The scene was grotesque. The grim atmosphere crept inside me. I was motionless. Time had stopped, but everyone else was moving forward. Their bodies were accelerating, moving faster than normal. The kid was dead. Hit by a car in front of the apartment complex.

The mother wasn't watching the kid and he ran into traffic in the parking lot. That's what had happened, and that's what the mother was going to have to live with.
I watched for a moment and then retreated back inside my

apartment. What did I do? I should have brought the kid down to his mother, and then everything would have been all right. Yeah. Everything would have been all right. But I didn't. I let the kid sit outside my door and cry, and I tried to block it out and blame the mother for not knowing where her kid was. I didn't think about the consequences

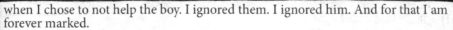

when I chose to not help the boy. I ignored them. I ignored him. And for that I am forever marked.

A few days passed and I found myself sitting in my room covered in blankets with the heat turned all the way up. It was hot as an oven. But I didn't notice. How could I?

I felt responsible for the death of that innocent child, and worst of all I had no one to tell. My wife wouldn't understand; after all, she was friends with the neighbor. How could I tell her what I had done? What would she say, let alone think?

No, it would be easier to isolate myself and pretend I was coming down with the flu. That's what I'll do. My constant vomiting must

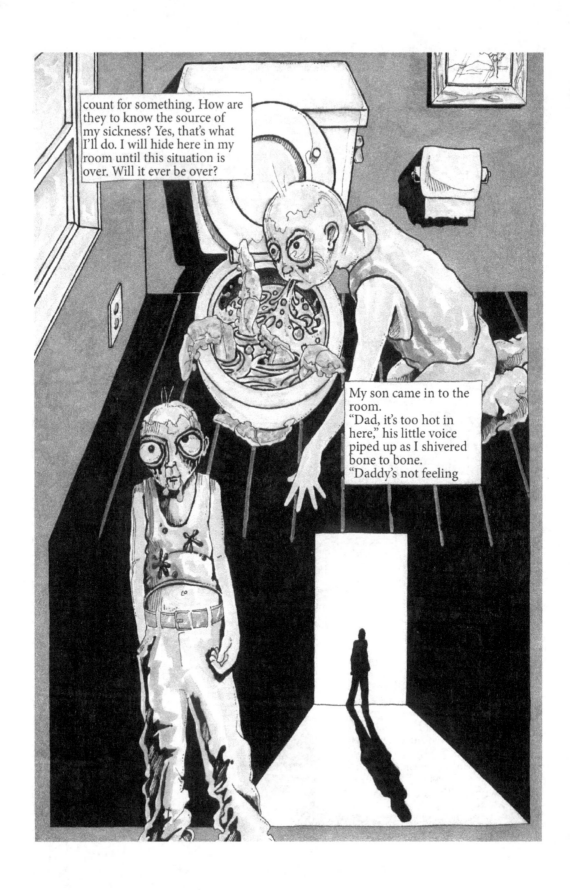

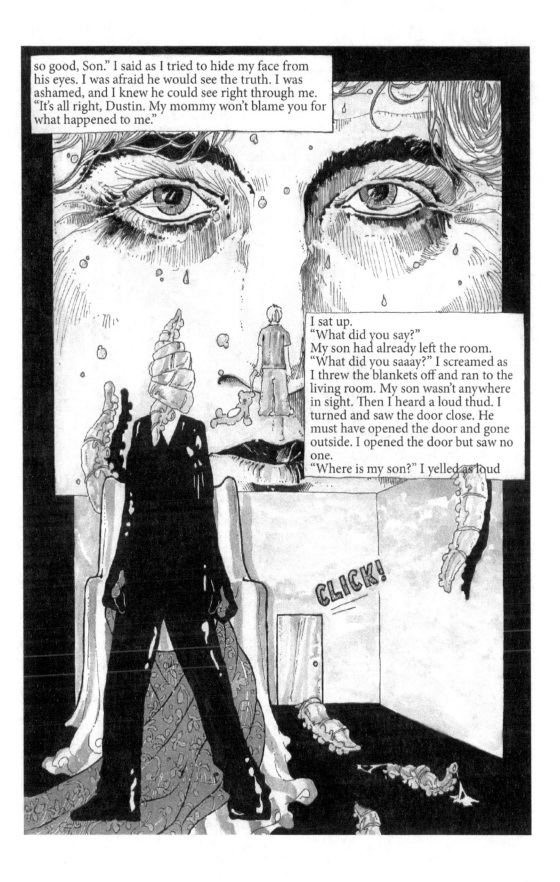

so good, Son." I said as I tried to hide my face from his eyes. I was afraid he would see the truth. I was ashamed, and I knew he could see right through me. "It's all right, Dustin. My mommy won't blame you for what happened to me."

I sat up.
"What did you say?"
My son had already left the room.
"What did you saaay?" I screamed as I threw the blankets off and ran to the living room. My son wasn't anywhere in sight. Then I heard a loud thud. I turned and saw the door close. He must have opened the door and gone outside. I opened the door but saw no one.
"Where is my son?" I yelled as loud

CLICK!

as I could. I looked down the stairwell and saw his little body making its way out the front door, toward the parking lot.

"Oh my God, no!" I tried to run down the stairwell, but my body seemed to move in slow motion. The faster I tried to run, the slower I moved. My mind raced ahead of my body until I finally reached the bottom of the stairs. I flung open the door and ran outside.

His little body was toddling across the parking lot; I knew what I had to do. No question about it this time. I ran into the parking lot to save my son from whatever killed the neighbor boy.

As I got closer, I felt the warmth inside my body leave as though it were taken. Numbness swept over me and replaced my soul with something else. Then the screeching stopped

and I found myself finally at peace.
As the first responders scraped my body off the asphalt and shoved it into
the black body bag, a little boy sat inside his downstairs apartment and
watched events unfold from his bedroom window. The closer to the glass
he was, the more distant he became. A smile formed on the little boy's face.
He was searching for his mother. Although he never found what he was
looking for, he had helped somebody else discover what he needed to find.

CHAPTER 4

DEACONS AVE.

Deacons Ave

story by
Dustin Warburton
art by
Jay Trefethen

It had finally stopped raining when David Thompson decided it was time for his evening jog. He climbed into his well-worn sweat pants. His wife was fast asleep. He kissed her on the cheek and walked out the front door. As he stretched on the grassy lawn outside his apartment, he looked at the sky. Stars were emerging through the clouds. The moon was full.

Every night David went for a run in order to burn off the stress from the day's activities. What better way to fall asleep than to climb into bed after a good run. The numbing sensation in your legs is extraordinary.

David had jogged a little over two miles from his home when the pit of his stomach suddenly cramped. "It'll go away

he told himself, can't stop now." He gripped his left
side. The cramp worsened, but David kept telling himself
he couldn't stop, no matter what.

While the sweat started to seep into David's eyes, the pain became excruciating. He had no other choice but to stop. His knees weak-
ened and he fell in the middle of the street. The cramps were like nothing he had ever felt before. He thrashed on the pavement in agony.

Then as suddenly as the cramps came, they were gone. David was
on his back when he realized the pain had disappeared. He rose to his
feet, confused about what had happened. For the pain to leave so quickly? What could it be? Food Poisoning? At that moment David tried to
get his bearings. He checked the street sign, gleaming with moonlight. Deacons Ave.

"Sir, you forgot your paper."

The voice echoed down the street. David turned and saw nothing, but knew he'd heard a voice. He looked up and down the street. Nothing.

"I must be hearing things." He shook his head and started walking home.

"Sir, you forgot your paper." This time the voice was louder than before. David jumped in surprise but still could see nothing.

"This has got to be a joke." David stooped and retied his shoelaces. That's when he noticed something ahead, reflected in the pave street. No more than ten feet away at the base of a streetlight was a shadowy figure, shaped like a person. David squinted and saw nothing but that strange apparition standing sideways.

"Sir, you forgot your paper." The voice was faint, but David heard it. He stood motionless and felt his eyes water. Then the shadow began to move toward him, almost hovering along the ground.

David shook his head and tried to recover his senses. The shadow was coming closer. David's hands began to shake. The shadow was only a few feet away. Just as David was about to run he felt an icy finger touch his shoulder.

David screamed. He sprinted away, headed for home. What was that impression in the street? Who was calling out to him? And what had touched his shoulder? These questions raced through his mind as quickly as David raced home.

As he reached the apartment complex, he sighed with relief. He must have been hallucinating. Maybe it was that cramp, or the lack of oxygen to the brain?

David laughed as he rationalized what had happened. Just as he opened the front door to his apartment he saw the newspaper on the

ground near the steps. His wife must have forgotten to bring it in.

David picked up the paper and glanced at the front page. He stopped and held the paper high. The front-page headline read,

15 YEAR OLD BOY DIES WHILE WORKING PAPER ROUTE

David scanned the article. On the previous day, a

young boy delivering newspapers was struck by a truck and killed. David suddenly shrieked in pain and fell to one knee, holding his side. The horrible cramps had come back, along with something else. David's eyes went blank and he collapsed. His crumpled body sprawled on the concrete steps to his apartment. Underneath his face was the newspaper. Directly under his eyelids were the words:

"The boy was struck and killed while riding his bike on Deacons Ave."

the end

Chapter 5

The Cursed Soul

I am about to tell you a story, an incident which occurred during my childhood. As Halloween grows near, so does the fear inside my body. As children prepare for a night of spooks and treats, some lock themselves indoors praying for dawn. An old man once said, "ghouls and goblins roam the countryside, Spirits of the deceased rise from their ancient slumber becoming mist in the night's sky. Evil awakens once a year, for the night of Halloween is finally here." These words haunt me from day to day.

It all began when I met the old man. The year was 1986. I was 15 years old. It was the evening of October 30th, a friend and I were on our way to the local library. Michael was friends with a weird old man who knew an awful lot about local folklore. We were hoping he could give us some ideas for Halloween. We entered the front door, I followed Mike into the basement of the library. When I entered the room the smell of dust and mildew was so overwhelming it almost made me sick. Books on the shelves looked as if they haven't been touched in fifty years.

"There he is," Mike pointed across the room. Low and behold, I saw a short pudgy old man with a straggly beard waving us over. We pulled up two chairs and sat next to him.

"Hello Michael."

"Hello sir," Mike said while shaking his hand.

"Who is this young seed you have brought to me?"

"This is my friend Dustin." I reached over and shook his hand. They were sweaty and cold as ice. Mike told the old man that we were doing a report in school on local folklore, and we needed his help. He didn't want to tell him our true intentions.

"Oh, I know a tale or two," the old man glared towards me.

"In the year 1886, 13 bodies were discovered in Chenango County during the month of October. All of the corpses were without heads, and some were stripped of their limbs. Locals began to suspect something evil was at work. On the night of October 30th, a hermit by the name of Thomas Ripley was caught trying to abduct a child on the streets of Norwich. He was beaten and taken into custody; he soon admitted to the murders. When he was asked why he had done such horrible crimes, Ripley simply answered, 'I needed their blood.'"

"The people of Norwich decided to rid this evil being from their township as soon as possible. The next day, Ripley was dragged up a cliff, which is located between Norwich and Oxford. He was beaten so bad his limbs were useless. On the very top of the cliff a grave was dug. He was placed inside a wooden box, it is said his screams were heard miles away. The only priest who was present spoke to Ripley. 'Do you have any last words before we put an end to your wretchedness?'

"While blood poured out of his mouth, he shouted out 'in time, as the soil fades and my coffin is revealed, my essence will be known. I shall return stronger and hungrier with hatred, which burns in all of you. You can not defeat me, I will have all of your children.'

" 'Get him in there,' the priest shouted with anger. Ripley laughed as the men pushed him back in. He was buried alive. All throughout the night, the sound of laughter was heard coming from his grave."

"His stone still remains near the edge of the cliff. In time, his coffin will shine through the crumbling rock, which is getting closer every year. Next time your traveling on East River Road on the way to Oxford, look out to your left. You might still be able to hear laughter in the nights sky, since tomorrow night is the 100th anniversary of his death."

The old man leaned back away from the table. He had an ungodly grin on his face. Our eyes met; no words were spoken but something was present. "Dustin," Mike grabbed my shoulder and pulled me out of my trancelike state. "We got to go," Mike apologized for our short stay, but thanked him for his eerie tale. I reached over to shake his hand, he looked at me like I had caught on to something.

As we were leaving I looked back, the old man whispered, "he sees you." Then smiled, revealing his blackened teeth. Mike had made up everything, there was no report, we didn't have to leave, Mike had already made his mind, We were going up to that grave on Halloween night for whatever sick and demented reason we could conjure up, that became our mission. Lucky for us it happened to be on a Saturday night, giving us the entire day to get ready.

That night I laid in bed feeling uneasy, I had the worst feeling something bad was going to happen. What scared me the most were those cold lifeless eyes I looked into. Wondering what was really in there. When I awoke, the smell of October rust was in the air. Sky was black as night, a cold chill swept over the land that unfaithful morning. During the course of the day we gathered all of our gear. Shovels, flashlights, pick, crowbar, axe. We ended up recruiting two more friends to join us on our quest. Brian, who was our age, and Jonathan. He was a few years older, a type of misfit among his age group. Lucky for us he had a truck, since the grave was about 20 miles away from where we lived.

As the sun went down, and the moon began to shine, the atmosphere of Hollow's Eve was clearly present to us as we drove through town. Tons of little monsters roamed the streets. Faces emerged from the pumpkins that glared at us through every window we passed. As we approached the site, Mike let Jon know we were there. We parked on the side of the road, the cliff was visible, but it was a mile hike through the forest to reach the bottom.

We reached the top of the cliff at 9:30. Nothing was visible to us. Weeds and bushes were overgrown making it impossible to find anything. I started walking through the brush, looking for anything that resembled a grave. We were about to give up when we heard Brian. "Guys, guys, get over here quick!" We rushed to his side; there in front of us lied an old stone cross. There was no name, or any type of markings of any sort. Instantly Mike started digging; I couldn't believe what we were doing. John and Brian joined in while I stood silent, emotionless along with an axe that hung from my right arm.

"Are you going to help?" Jon demanded from me. I did not reply.

"Forget him, I knew he would back out, just remember we're in this together." Brian yelled to me with a snobby tone. "Sure, we're all in this together," I thought to my self.

An old apple tree looked over us kind of like the night watchman. Its branches hung in all directions, looking almost like an old bony hand ready to devour us. Suddenly Mike cried out, "It's here." We all knelt down around the coffin. We brushed away the remaining soil; I was surprised in how good of shape the coffin was. Mike pried it open with the crowbar, and got it loose. Before opening it, we all looked at one another, then without hesitation the cover was off. I stood up, body shaking, sweat pouring from my scalp. "What have we done?"

We expected to find a skeleton, but what we found was much worse. The moment the moonlight hit the body a change began. The evil inside ourselves started to rise, creating a new type of existence. It was then I knew what I had to do.

The next thing I knew, the four of us were running frantically through the woods- everyone screaming as if something was chasing us. I still remember hearing their cries echo throughout the dark. One by one, the cries faded, until all was

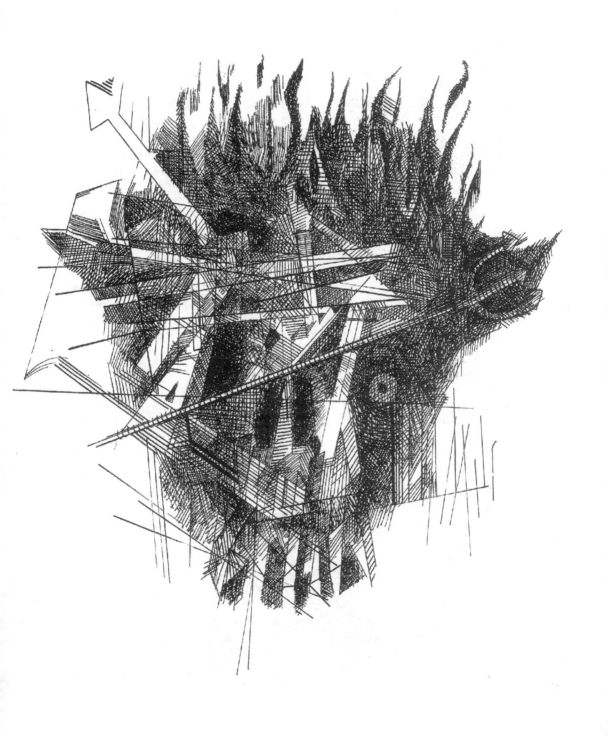

silent. I realized I was alone, the last one left. I still had the axe gripped tightly in my right hand. Blood was dripping from my hands, I must have cut myself somehow. For some reason I had no fear. Whatever it was out there was stalking me, I could feel it inside of me. I had no idea what was happening, all I knew was it had already gotten my friends. I crouched down underneath a pine tree and waited for it to come. It wasn't going to get me that easy, not without a fight.

The morning of November 1st one of the search parties found me sitting near the grave. I was covered in blood while holding Michael's head in my arms. Michael's body was found over two miles away. All three bodies were found that morning, only one of then without a head. I soon realized I had killed my friends for no apparent reason. All of then were hacked up, found within a couple hundred yards of each other. When they asked me why I murdered my friends, what made me do it. I told them," I did not kill anyone, nor hurt them. I simply showed them what they wanted to see."

So here I sit in my padded cell confined to a straight jacket for the last fourteen years, wondering what happens next. Funny how evil shows up now and then to let you know it really exists. Soon enough the time will come. I will sit here and eat the pudding they shove down my throat, play their mind games and speak to their doctors. For when the time comes it will happen all over again. Some poor fool will speak to the old man and he will send them to where they need to go. Like I said before. It all began when I looked into those cold lifeless eyes of the old man.

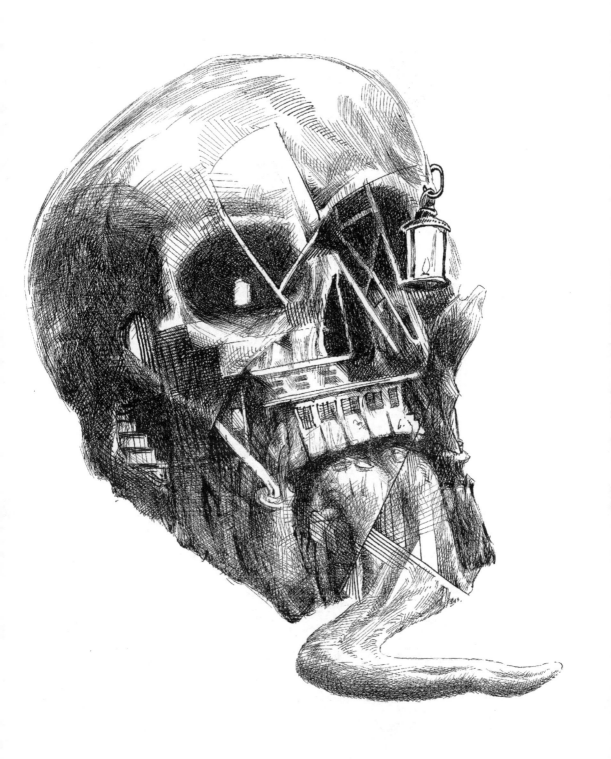

CHAPTER 6

FACELESS

Faceless

Story by Dustin Warburton

Art by Jay Trefethen

Ever since I was a little boy, I've had strange dreams about a man in black. He always appears with

a shadow covering his face. His dark figure haunts my thoughts to this day. Even as a grown man I cannot escape his touch. Only when I am sleeping does he appear. I know this sounds like a copycat Freddy Kruger, but this is no movie.

I can still remember the first time I met him. I was 12 years old. My mother and father had bought a new station wagon. Tinted windows, sunroof, electric seats: the world had stopped and finally my father had something to brag about. No more being stranded on the side of the road as police cruisers stopped so the cops could pull my drunken father out of the car. Not anymore. We were cruising in style. Inheriting a small amount of money from a relative can alter one's lifestyle in fantastic ways.

The smell of a new car was different from anything I was used to. I didn't see the multicolored mold that used to infest the carpets in the back seat of our old Chevy. And I didn't hear the mice that used to crawl inside its door panels and gnaw the speaker wires. This was supposed to be a good night for our family, and I remember it well.

My father said we were going out to dinner. I had no idea where we were going. Just the fact that we were going somewhere—hell, I had never left the town, let alone gone out to dinner in a restaurant. The closest I ever got to eating out was when I had surgery in the hospital and I was served food in my bed for three days. That was great, but not as exciting as

going out to a restaurant.

My mother's curly hair waved back and forth in the cool wind. Her window was open due to the stench of plastic. I never thought a new car would smell so foul.

"We just have to break it in, won't take long," my father said as he guzzled his beer and threw the can out the window. It wouldn't take him long; already garbage was accumulating on the front dash.

The sun was down when we began our journey; the night was setting in deeper and faster as we traveled farther from home. The moon was shining more powerfully than I had ever seen it. As I stared

into the black craters of its surface, I felt a chill. I looked around in a panic. A field bordered both sides of the road. I could see far into the landscape due to the brightness of the moonlight. A tractor was visible in the distance, surrounded by bushes and weeds. Sitting on the tractor was a dark figure concealed in shadows.

My eyes were deceiving me. I rubbed them and looked again. It was gone. I sat back in my seat and took a deep breath. No more horror films for me.

I laughed.

"What was that, son?" My father's grip tight-

ened on the steering wheel.

   "Nothing, Dad. I just thought I saw something out in that field, but it was nothing."

   "That's good to hear. I wouldn't want you to be scared." His voice was somehow different. His hands were now off the steering wheel.

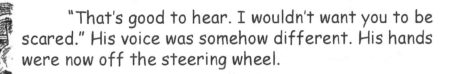

   "Dad, what are you doing?" My head was pounding, trying to catch up with my thoughts.

   He turned toward me, and it wasn't my father. Its hair was the same and the clothes were the same, but the face was gone: there was nothing left but

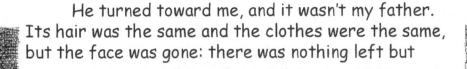

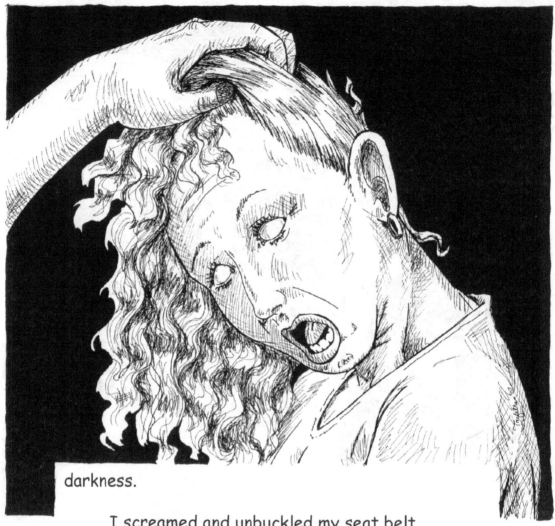

darkness.

I screamed and unbuckled my seat belt.

"What's the matter, son? Don't you like what you see, isn't it what you wanted?"

I screamed at my mother. "Mom, tell him to stop, please tell him to stop!" Tears flowed from my swelling eyes.

There was no answer. My mother was gone, although her body was still in the seat. Her spirit had been taken, snatched by this horrible figure in the driver's seat of my father's new car. The face-less phantom grabbed my mother's head and brought

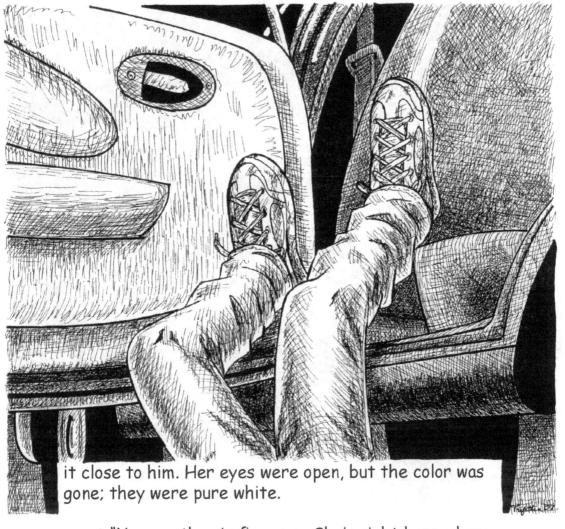

it close to him. Her eyes were open, but the color was gone; they were pure white.

"Your mother is fine, son. She's right here where she should be." The creature started wiggling her head so it bobbled up and down, lifeless as a doll. "She's nothing more than a useless slab of flesh," he said as I cried uncontrollably.

I pulled the door handle and jumped out of the car, hoping to get away.

I fell to the ground violently but felt no pain. As I rose to my feet, the car stopped; inside the phantom was still. His faceless expression bored through my soul. I was unable to think, unable to comprehend what

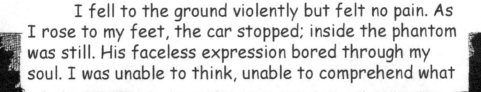

was happening. This has to be a dream, this has to be a dream, I told myself as I covered my eyes.

"This is no dream," the voice said from behind me. I jumped and turned but saw no one. I looked toward the car, and the car was gone. My eyes drifted up and down the landscape. I was alone.

Then I heard a noise. The sound of a tractor starting up. I couldn't believe what was happening, and worst of all I was alone in an unfamiliar place, away from my parents. I didn't know where I was and I fell to the ground.

The sound of the tractor grew closer as I curled into a ball and hoped that God would save

me from this nightmare. Then the noise stopped. I snapped out of my frantic state of mind and rose to my feet. The tractor was a few yards away from where I was standing. The bushes and weeds covering it were gone. The figure was nowhere to be found. I looked all over, waiting for it to reappear and frighten me again. But it didn't. The only thing I could hear was the distant howling of coy dogs in search of dinner.

I walked to the tractor and stood near its rusted metal frame. I walked around it many times but saw nothing and heard no one. Then I climbed up the side and sat on the cold metal seat, which was warm from its previous driver. I felt powerful. I didn't feel as alone as I had been only minutes ago. Then I saw

our car in the distance: its lights shined far ahead on
the road. The headlights approached as I sat motionless on the tractor and watched the spectators come
closer, closer to me and they weren't even aware of my
presence. I wondered what it was and why it had come
when it did. Then I realized what it was and why it had
come; the only thing I didn't know was when I would
see him again.

"What was that, son?" My father's grip tight-
ened on the steering wheel.

"Nothing, Dad, I just thought I saw something
out in that field, but it was nothing." I looked out the
window again.

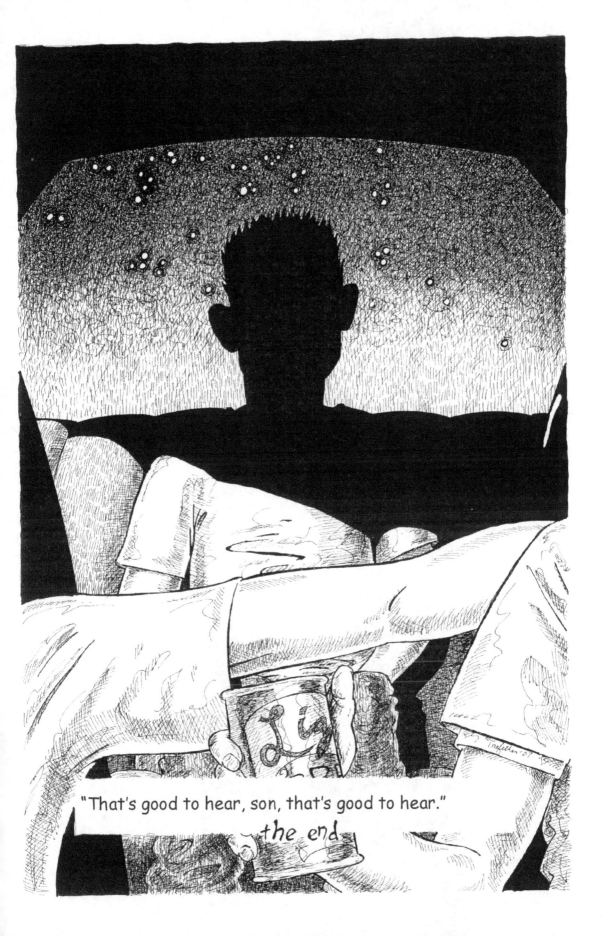

Gallery of
Steven Blickenstaff

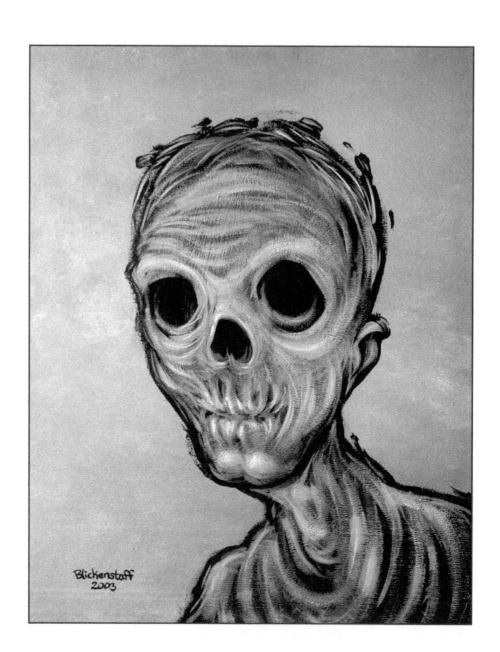

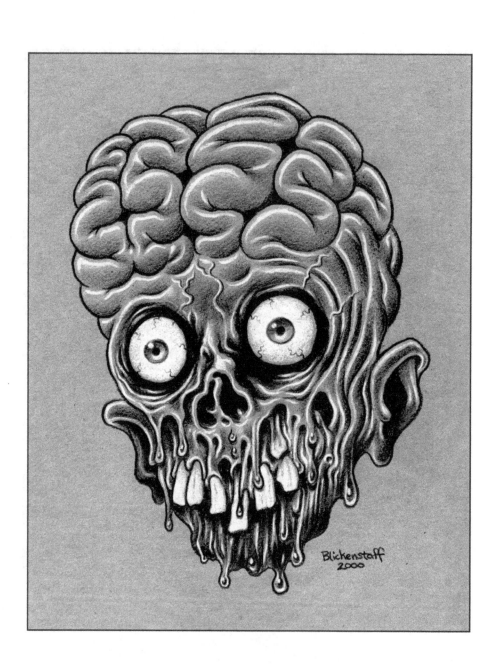

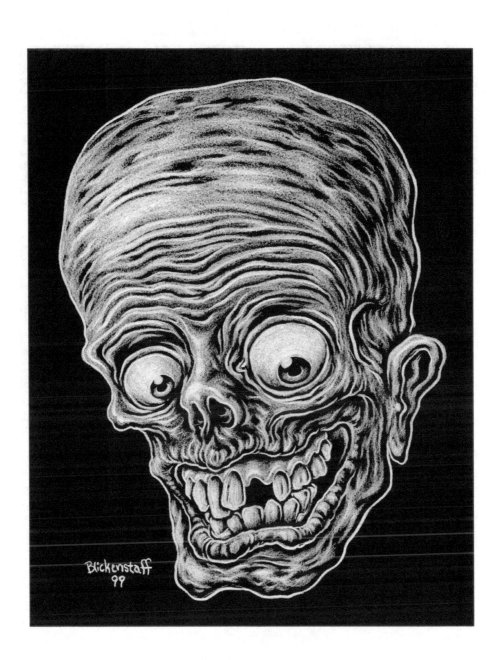

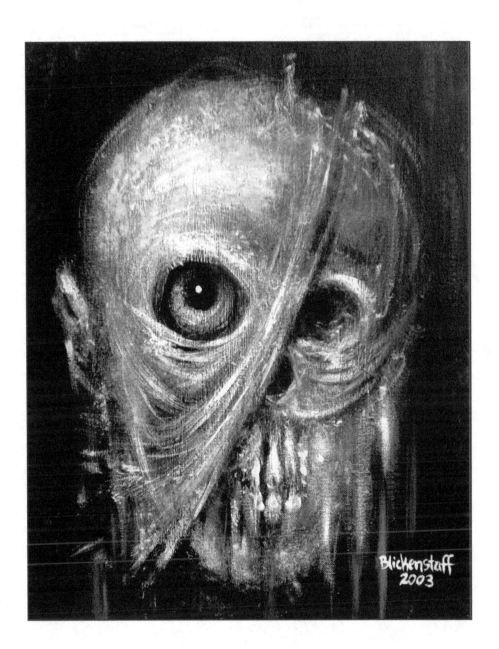

GALLERY OF
JOHN EDWARD BONAVENTURE FEDEROWICZ

ILLUSTRATIONS of a LIFETIME

BON
FED
PRODUCTIONS

GALLERY OF
FRANK RUSSO

GALLERY OF
JAY TREFETHEN

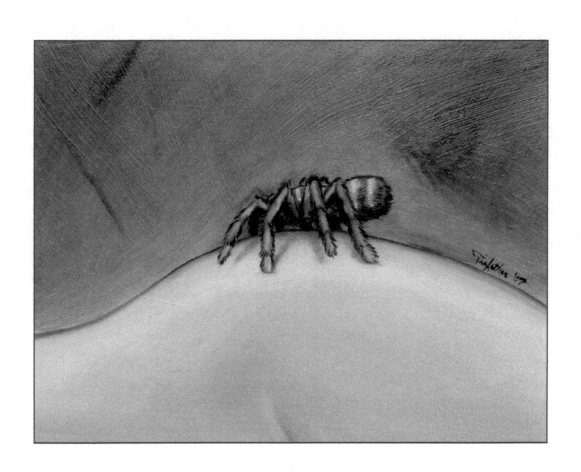

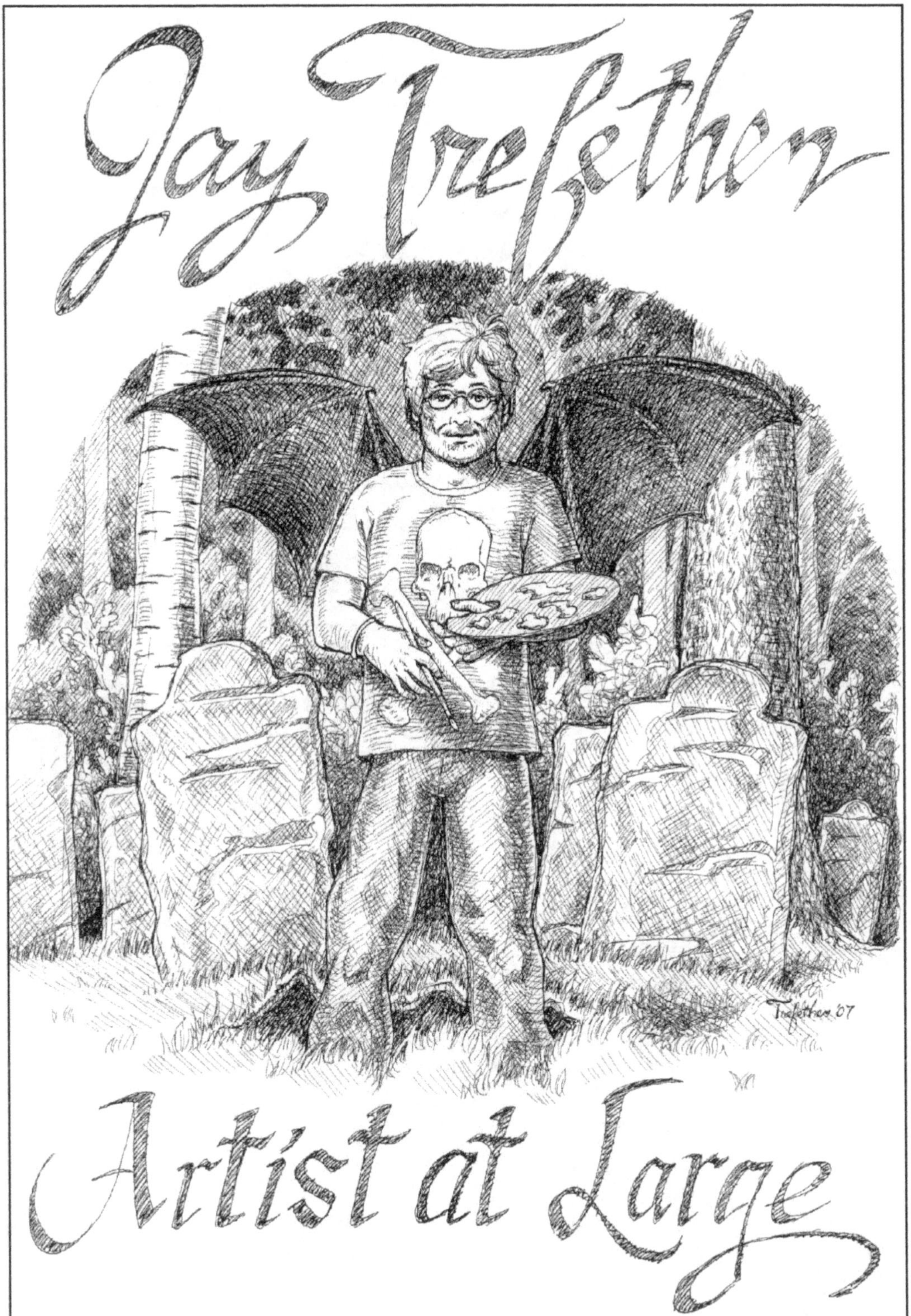
Jay Trefethen
Trefethen '07
Artist at Large

GALLERY OF
NATHAN GORMAN

Gallery of
Kevin Clement

CPSIA information can be obtained
at www.ICGtesting.com
Printed in the USA
BVHW061002180521
607553BV00007B/951